A KIDS CAN CHOOSE BOOK

Willy's Noisy Sister

WRITTEN BY ELIZABETH CRARY ▪ ILLUSTRATED BY SUSAN AVISHAI

Parenting Press, Inc.
SEATTLE, WASHINGTON

First edition
Printed in the United States of America

Book design by Margarite Hargrave

Library of Congress Cataloging-in-Publication Data

Crary, Elizabeth, 1942-
Willy's noisy sister / written by Elizabeth Crary ; illustrated by Susan Avishai.
p. cm. – (A kids can choose book)
ISBN 1-884734-58-8 (lib. bdg.) – ISBN 1-884734-57-X (pbk.)
1. Problem solving in children–Juvenile literature. 2. Brothers and sisters–Juvenile literature.
[1. Problem solving. 2. Brothers and sisters.] I. Avishai, Susan, ill. II. Title.

BF723.P8 C75 2001
153.4'3–dc21 00-062391

Note to Parents, Teachers, and Caregivers

When a child faces a frustrating situation, the more ideas he or she considers, the more appropriate his or her behavior is likely to be.

The "Kids Can Choose" books model a process for solving problems and offer a variety of ways children can respond. Each book in this series explores a common problem for children, such as nonviolent teasing, theft of personal belongings, and personal space encroachment.

In each story some choices are successful and others are not–this helps children realize that they may need to try *several* strategies before they find one that works. The characters also model reflecting on various options *before they act.*

How to Use These Books

Read the story and let your child make the choices. When you come to a box (■) read the question and wait while your child responds. Accept his or her responses without correction or criticism. You can ask your child to elaborate with questions like "Why do you think that worked?" or "Have you ever tried something like that?"

Transition from Story to Real Life

It takes more than reading these books several times for children to be able to apply the principles to real life. Children need to practice using the approach in non-stressful situations. The following five steps make the transfer easier:

1. Act out the situation in the book with other kids or adults.
2. Brainstorm new ideas and add them to the list on page 30.
3. Pick five ideas (one for each finger) and act them out with an imaginary problem.
4. Choose five ideas for a past problem and act them out.
5. Ask your child to list different ways to handle a current problem and act them out.

When children can use the approach in non-stressful situations, you can remind them they have options in real life. For example, you could say, "What options have you considered?" or, for children who are reluctant to talk about their issues, "What might Willy have done in a situation like yours?"

Through these books you are helping your child learn to make smart decisions. Keep the tone light and ***have fun!***

Elizabeth Crary
Seattle, Washington

Willy came into the house slowly. He looked around and listened carefully. The house was quiet.

Maya, his little sister, must still be napping. “Hooray!” he thought to himself. “I need some peace and quiet after that bus ride home.”

Willy had a problem. His ears were too good! He could always hear what the teacher said, as well as the secrets kids whispered at school. Loud noises actually hurt his ears. The bus ride home from school was especially noisy today. Everyone was so excited that it was Friday.

Willy pulled out his toy animals. He wanted to be a veterinarian when he grew up. He liked to talk to his animals. As he was setting up the horses, he heard Maya jumping on her bed. "Oh, no!" he thought, "Maya's up."

Willy wondered what to do. Maya was fun, but she was also noisy. She would soon show up in the living room, but he needed some quiet before he played with her.

"I can go to my room," he thought, "but I don't want to.

"Dad always says it's easier to distract Maya than deal with her, but that works for him because he has lots of ideas.

"I could ask Mom for help, but she will ask me what I've tried. She'll probably suggest I offer Maya choices or make a deal with her. Why can't that kid just leave me alone?"

Before Willy could decide what to do, Maya was standing in front of him, commanding, "Play with me!"

"Later, Maya," Willy replied. "Right now I want to play by myself."

"Now, now, NOW!" Maya demanded, as she bounced on Willy's back.

Willy winced at the noise. "I need quiet for ten minutes, then I will play with you. Will you ask Mom to set the timer for ten minutes and play by yourself until it rings?"

"No. I wan-na play NOW."

Willy covered his ears and reviewed his choices, as Maya chanted, "Now, now, NOW."

■ What do you think Willy will try first?

Distract Maya 10
Move to his room 12
Offer two choices 18
Make a deal with Maya 20
Change the situation 26

(Wait for child to respond after each question. Look at page 3, "Note to Parents, Teachers, and Caregivers," for ways to encourage children to think for themselves.)

10 Distract Maya

"How can I distract Maya?" Willy moaned.

"Dad says to involve her in what I'm doing or suggest something fun for her to do. Let me think. Maya likes to draw, so I could ask her to draw a picture for me," he thought.

"Maya, will you draw a picture for me?"

"No. I want to be with you," she stated emphatically.

"You can use my special marking pens," he offered.

Maya paused a moment, considering, then agreed. Willy gave her his marking pens and paper. She went off to draw at the kitchen table.

Five minutes later Maya was back. "See my picture?" she said proudly.

"That's nice," Willy said. He wailed to himself, "My ears still hurt. What can I do now? I still need more quiet time."

■ What do you think Willy will try next?

Move to his room 12

Ask for help 24

12 Move to his room

Willy scooped up his animals and tromped off to his room. "I don't want to play in my room, but at least it will be quieter," he grumbled to himself.

He closed the door and put his animals down. Before he sat down, Maya was knocking on his door, saying, "I wan-na play with you."

Willy sighed in frustration. His noisy sister wasn't in his room, but her voice was. He really wanted some peace and quiet.

"Should I let her in or ignore her," he fussed. "If I don't let her in, she might go away or she might keep knocking until dinner. If I do let her in, she might be a pest or she might be quiet."

Willy sat on the floor with his animals and thought about what to do.

■ What do you think Willy will try next?

Ignore Maya *14*

Look for the bright side *16*

14 Ignore Maya

Willy decided to ignore Maya's knocking.

"If I can ignore her for five minutes, maybe she'll give up and leave me alone," he moaned to himself, as Maya continued to knock on his door.

"It sure is hard to ignore that noise," he fumed as he covered his ears. "How can I stop the sound?"

"I know. I'll cover my head with a pillow." He picked up a book and lay down on his bed. He covered his ears with the pillow and began to read.

Shortly, the knocking stopped. Willy listened. It sounded like Maya was gone. "Great!" he thought.

Cautiously, he got off the bed and sat down by his animals. His room was still quiet. He sighed in relief and began to play with his animals.

The End

■ How do you like this ending?

16 Look for the bright side

"Dad always says when things look grim, look for the bright side. I think I need to look for the bright side before I let Maya in," muttered Willy. He picked up a horse and asked, "What can the bright side of a noisy sister be?"

"Well, first," Willy thought, "Maya likes me. Whenever Mom or Dad get mad at me, she comes and slips her hand into mine. It doesn't change things, but it is nice.

"And she misses me when I'm at school. I guess that's why she wants to play with me when I get home. Maybe if I read her a story first, she'll let me be by myself — and that is certainly a bright idea."

Willy opened the door and asked, "Maya, would you like me to read you a story?" Maya nodded her head. "Okay, go get a picture book, and we'll read it together."

Maya was back in a flash. They sat down on the floor near the animals and talked about the pictures in the book.

"Well," Willy thought, "reading to Maya can be fun. I'm not alone, but at least she is quiet."

The End

■ How do you like this ending?

18 Offer two choices

Willy decided to offer Maya some ideas. His older cousin, Andrew, said the best choices are things that are fun. "So, what would be fun for Maya?" he fretted.

"She has a lot of energy. Maybe she would like to jump on her bed or dance. And she likes doing everything I do. So maybe she would like to build a farm for my animals with blocks."

Willy sat up straight and looked at his sister. He took a deep breath and began, "Maya, I want to be alone. I will play with you in ten minutes. You can dance in your room or build a farm for my animals while you wait for me."

Maya's face clouded up as if she were going to say, "No." Willy hurriedly added, "In ten minutes I will play what you want. We can play chase or put my animals in the farm you build."

Maya thought for a moment and then smiled, "Okay," and ran off.

Willy sighed and reached for his animals. "Peace and quiet at last," he said.

Turn to page 28.

20 Make a deal

Willy decided to make a deal. To make a fair deal he needed to find an idea they both liked and a way that worked for both of them.

"Maya," he said, "let's make a deal. Okay?

"School was very noisy, and I want to play by myself for a long while. You want me to play now, right?" Maya nodded. "What will work for both of us?"

"You play now," Maya replied.

"That is your idea, Maya," Willy explained. "What is a new idea?"

Maya tilted her head one way, then the other as she thought. Finally she said, "You play soon."

"I will set the timer for ten minutes. When it rings, we can play. Okay?" he asked. Maya nodded.

"All right then, let's shake on the deal." They shook hands, and Willy set the timer and gave it to Maya.

Turn to page 28.

22 Do the unexpected

Willy grumbled to himself, “I don’t want to play anything noisy, but if she is quiet she can stay. If I give her something quiet to do, maybe she won’t bother me.”

“Maya, quick, sit down and help me take care of the baby cow. It’s sick,” he said as he pushed a calf toward her. “Its mother is gone and it needs someone to sing quietly to it and rub its back. If you want, you could even get a doll blanket and make a bed for it.”

Maya looked at the cow. “Why is it sick?” she asked.

“I don’t know,” Willy answered. “If you take care of her, I’ll try to find out. Remember to be quiet. Loud noises hurt sick cows. Shhh.”

Willy smiled as he watched his sister stroke the calf’s back. He wasn’t alone, but at least Maya was almost quiet.

The End

■ How do you like this ending?

24 Ask for help

Willy's ears still hurt. He decided to ask his mother for help. He went to the kitchen and pleaded, "Mom, make Maya be quiet. Please, please, please. She's hurting my ears and she won't leave me alone."

"What have you tried?" Mom inquired.

"I told her I needed quiet and asked her to let me play by myself for ten minutes. She said 'No.' Then I asked her to draw a picture for me, but she came back too fast."

"If I play with Maya now, will you play with her when ten minutes are up?" Mom asked.

"Yes. And thank you, Mom," Willy said, as he ran off to set the timer.

Turn to page 28.

26 Change the situation

Maya continued to chant, "Now, now, NOW."

"I wish Maya had a volume knob so I could turn her noise down," Willy fumed to himself. He imagined how it would look in place of her nose or her mouth.

"Or maybe I could have a sound shield so that her noise wouldn't bother me," he thought.

"Maybe I could make a sort of sound shield," he mused.

"I know what I can do," he thought excitedly. "I can use my ear plugs from swimming class."

He went to get them and Maya followed, chanting behind him. He put the plugs in and they helped. He could still hear her, but the sound was softer.

He continued to play with Maya chanting beside him. Finally, he decided he would make a deal or do something unexpected so he could have some real quiet.

■ What do you think Willy will try next?

Make a deal 20
Do something unexpected 22

Willy's quiet time was over and he felt better. He could deal with Maya and her noise now.

He set aside his animals and went to find her. She was building a barnyard with blocks. "I'm ready to play now. What would you like to do?" he asked her.

"I wan-na play animals with you," she smiled.

"Okay. You finish making the farm, and I'll get my animals."

He returned with the animals. "You can play with these," Willy said, as he gave her half the animals, "and I'll play with these. Let's pretend we have a dairy with the cows and a race track with the horses."

The End

■ How do you like this ending?

Idea page

Willy's ideas

- Ask Maya to leave him alone
- Distract Maya
- Move to his room
- Ignore Maya
- Look for the bright side
- Give two choices
- Make a deal
- Do the unexpected
- Ask for help
- Change the situation

Your ideas

■

■

■

■

■

■

■

■

■

■

■

■

■

Solving social problems . . .

Children's Problem Solving Books teach children to think about their problems. Each interactive story allows the reader to choose the main character's actions and see what happens as a result. Useful with 3–8 years. 32 pages, illustrated. $6.95 each. Written by Elizabeth Crary, illustrated by Marina Megale.

Solving interpersonal problems . . .

Kids Can Choose Books teach children to think about problems they may have with other children. Each interactive story allows the reader to choose the main character's actions and see what happens as a result. Useful with 5-10 years. 32 pages, illustrated. $7.95 each. Written by Elizabeth Crary, illustrated by Susan Avishai.

Someone is stealing Amy's pickle. What can she do?

Willy needs some peace and quiet. His sister wants to play–NOW! What can he do?

One of Heidi's classmates always snatches her hat off her head. What can she do?

Coping with intense feelings . . .

Dealing with Feelings Books acknowledge six intense feelings. Children discover safe and creative ways to express them. Each interactive story allows the reader to choose the main character's actions and see what happens as a result. Useful with 3-9 years. 32 pages, illustrated. $6.95 each. Written by Elizabeth Crary, illustrated by Jean Whitney.

Facing life's challenges . . .

The Decision Is Yours Books offer realistic dilemmas commonly faced by young people. Readers choose from among several alternatives to solve the problem. If they don't like the result of one solution, they can try a different one. Useful with 7-11 years. 64 pages, illustrated. $5.95 each. Various authors, illustrated by Rebekah Strecker.

Leader's Guide ($14.95) written by Carl Bosch offers activities that allow children to talk about values, ethics, feelings, safety, problem solving, and understanding behavior.

Library-bound editions available. Call Parenting Press, Inc. at **1-800-992-6657** for information about these and other helpful books for children and adults.

Prices subject to change without notice.